Princess Charlotte's
Picture Puzzles

An Exiting Day Trip

Princess Charlotte's
Picture Puzzles

An Exiting Day Trip

BOOKS

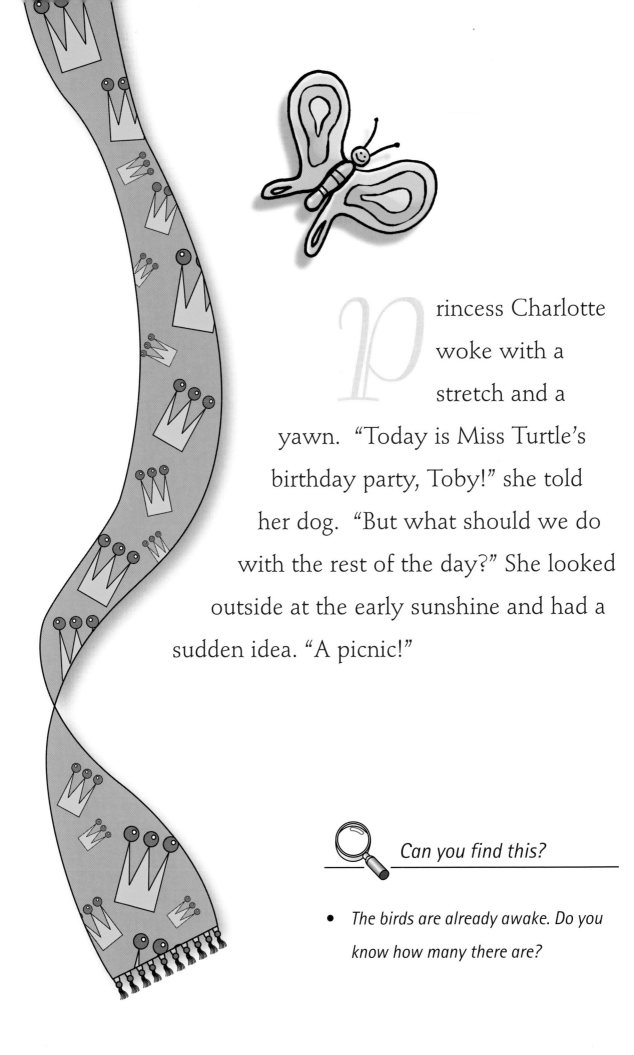

Princess Charlotte woke with a stretch and a yawn. "Today is Miss Turtle's birthday party, Toby!" she told her dog. "But what should we do with the rest of the day?" She looked outside at the early sunshine and had a sudden idea. "A picnic!"

Can you find this?

_____

- *The birds are already awake. Do you know how many there are?*

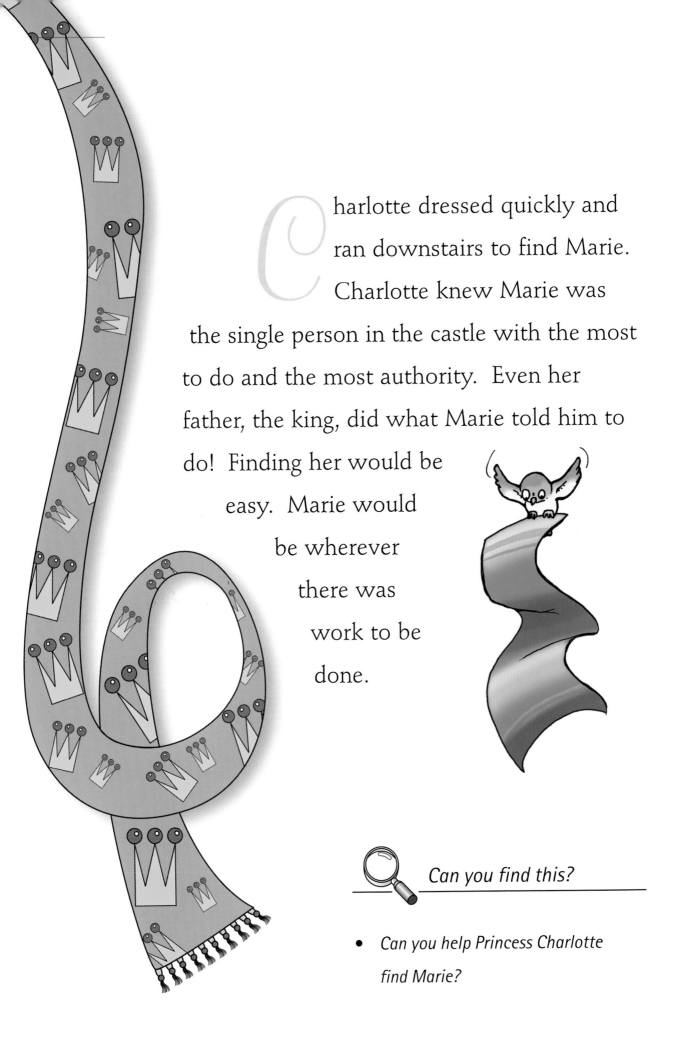

Charlotte dressed quickly and ran downstairs to find Marie. Charlotte knew Marie was the single person in the castle with the most to do and the most authority. Even her father, the king, did what Marie told him to do! Finding her would be easy. Marie would be wherever there was work to be done.

Can you find this?

- *Can you help Princess Charlotte find Marie?*

Charlotte made sure she ate a good breakfast and helped with the dishes before she asked Marie for her help with the picnic. Marie loved the idea. Together they made a list of things to pack and sent messages to each of Charlotte's friends, inviting them along.

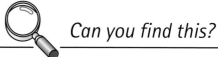

Can you find this?

- *Do you know how many pieces of fruit there are lying in the fruit dish?*

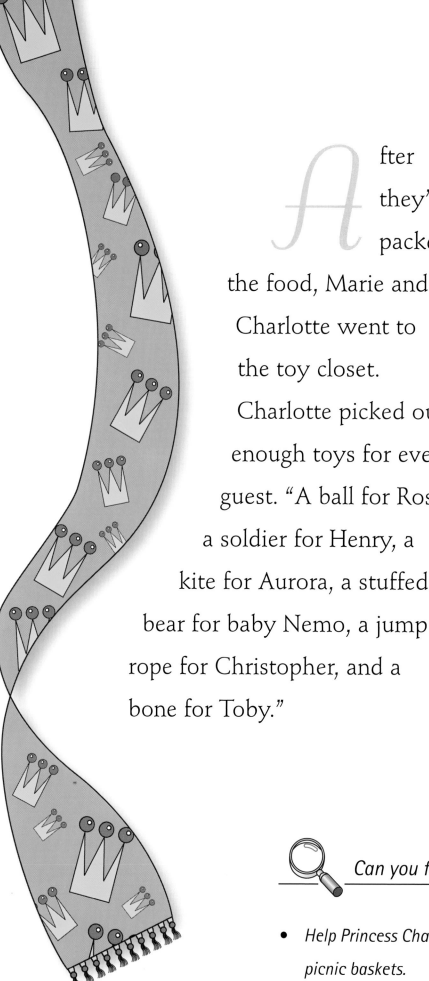

After they'd packed the food, Marie and Charlotte went to the toy closet. Charlotte picked out enough toys for every guest. "A ball for Rose, a soldier for Henry, a kite for Aurora, a stuffed bear for baby Nemo, a jump rope for Christopher, and a bone for Toby."

 Can you find this?

- *Help Princess Charlotte find all the picnic baskets.*

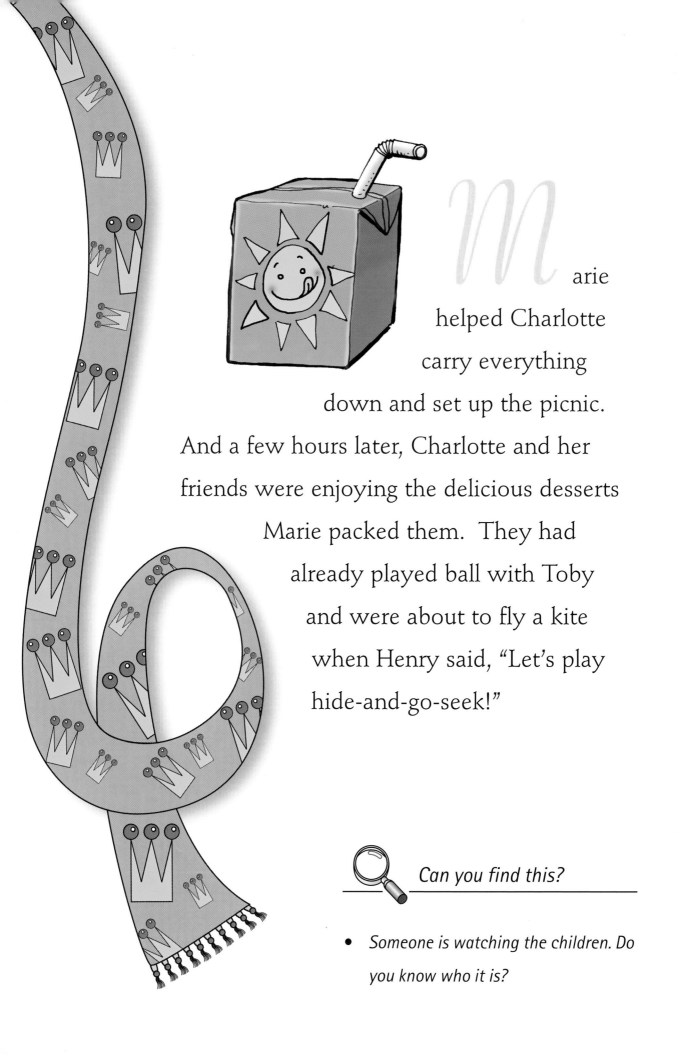

Marie helped Charlotte carry everything down and set up the picnic. And a few hours later, Charlotte and her friends were enjoying the delicious desserts Marie packed them. They had already played ball with Toby and were about to fly a kite when Henry said, "Let's play hide-and-go-seek!"

Can you find this?

- _Someone is watching the children. Do you know who it is?_

hey decided Toby should hide while they all looked for him. "One, Two, Three…" they counted as they closed their eyes. They looked and looked for Toby but couldn't find him. Charlotte was beginning to worry when she heard something.

"It's Toby!" she said, and she and her friends ran to find him.

Can you find this?

_____

- *Can you spot Toby in the picture?*

J ust then Toby poked his head out from behind the tree. The children were so glad to see him they almost didn't notice the little owl who fluttered down from the trees and landed on Charlotte's arm. He looked at her and then flapped up into the air before sailing off and calling to them, "You-whooo!"

Can you find this?

- *Can you find the three bags with nuts that are hidden in the picture?*

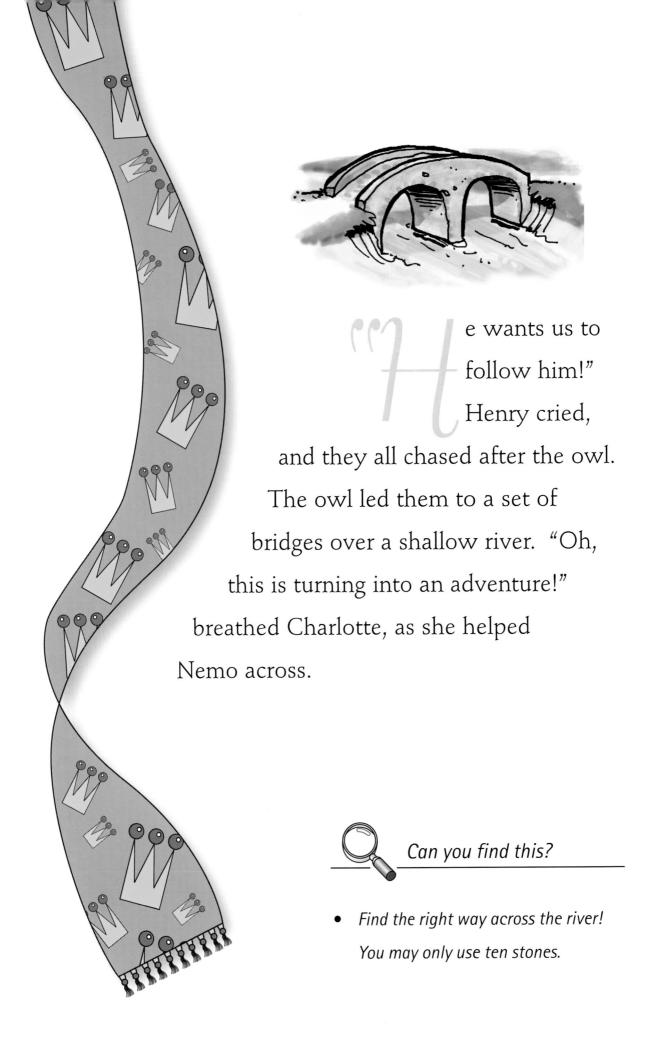

"He wants us to follow him!" Henry cried, and they all chased after the owl. The owl led them to a set of bridges over a shallow river. "Oh, this is turning into an adventure!" breathed Charlotte, as she helped Nemo across.

Can you find this?

- *Find the right way across the river! You may only use ten stones.*

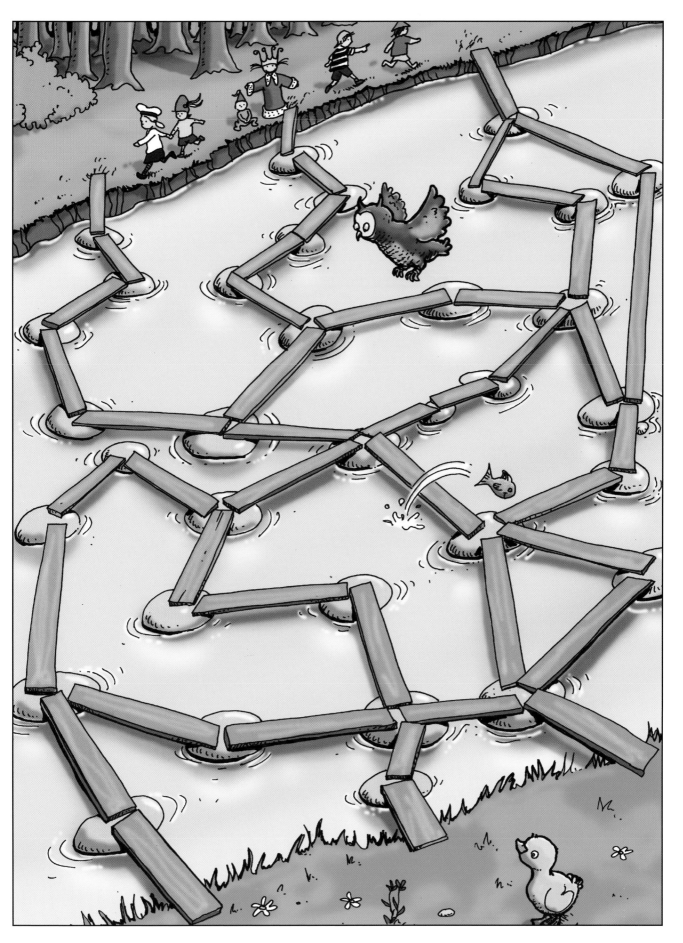

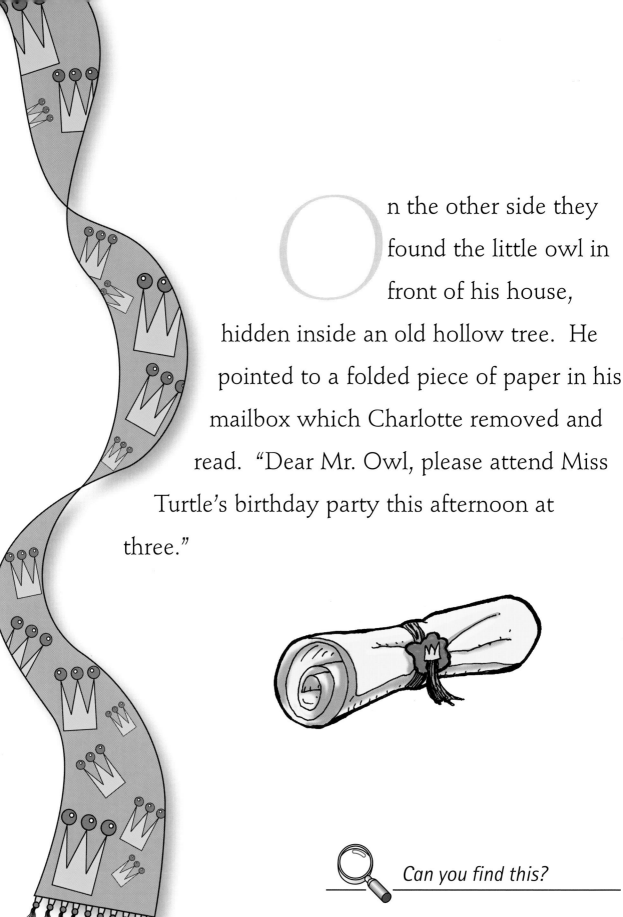

On the other side they found the little owl in front of his house, hidden inside an old hollow tree. He pointed to a folded piece of paper in his mailbox which Charlotte removed and read. "Dear Mr. Owl, please attend Miss Turtle's birthday party this afternoon at three."

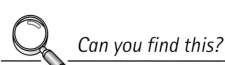

Can you find this?

- *Help the little owl to find his glasses and his bowtie.*

"I almost forgot, we have a party to go to!" Charlotte said. The children yelled and cheered because they loved parties. Suddenly, all sorts of creatures began emerging from their hiding places in the woods.

Can you find this?

- *Do you know how many children and how many animals there are?*

They had a wonderful time that day, sharing the rest of their desserts and getting to know all of their new friends. Charlotte helped Miss Turtle open her presents and they all danced so much they were exhausted.

Can you find this?

- *Can you name all the musical instruments on the picture?*

$f$inally they said goodnight to all of their friends and began to walk home. Mr. Owl made sure they knew the way and sailed off when they'd safely reached Charlotte's door. As he left they heard him call one last time, "Nice to meet you-whooo!"

Can you find this?

- *How many stars can you count?*

arie helped them get their pyjamas on and listened to them tell their stories about all they'd seen and done that day. Then she led them up to bed. She looked at them, smiled, and said, "My, my, Charlotte, but you did indeed have a very busy day!"

 Can you find this?

- *Can you find out which bed belongs to each child?*

Princess Charlotte

An Exiting Day Trip

Solutions

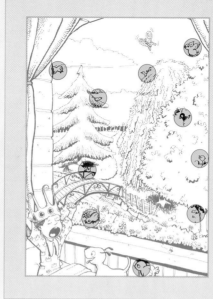

There are 10 birds in this drawing.

In this picture you can find where Marie is.

On the fruit dish there are 12 pieces of fruit.

There are 3 picnic baskets on the shelves.

A rabbit is looking at the playing children.

This picture shows you where Toby has hidden himself.

Princess Charlotte

An Exiting Day Trip
Solutions

This picture shows you where the three bags are hidden.

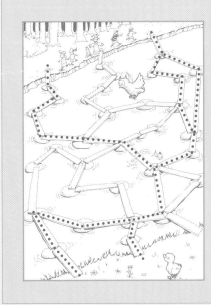

There are 3 possible ways to cross the river.

This picture shows you where to find the glasses and the bowtie.

There are 6 children and 29 animals.

Princess Charlotte

An Exiting Day Trip
Solutions

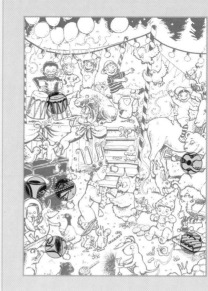

In this
drawing you
find:

a drum,
a piano,
a tuba,
a trumpet,
a xylophone
and a guitar.

There are
22 stars.

The numbers
show you
which bed
belongs to
which child.

© Yoyo Books, Geel, Belgium
www.yoyo-books.com
All rights reserved. Printed in Germany.
D-MM-II-8520-468